This book is dedicated to my mother, who is affectionately called Tootie, and who continually encourages my writing. – J. Samia Mair

ZAK and His Little LIES
First published in 2018 by THE ISLAMIC FOUNDATION
Distributed by
KUBE PUBLISHING LTD
Tel +44 (01530) 249230, Fax +44 (01530) 249656
E-mail: info@kubepublishing.com
Website: www.kubepublishing.com

Note to Parents and Teachers

Please note that an asterisk* has been used in the text to indicate where Muslims should say a blessing after mentioning the name of the Prophet Muhammad* (peace and blessings be upon him).

Author J. Samia Mair
Illustrator Omar Burgess
Book design Nasir Cadir
Editor Yosef Smyth

A Cataloguing-in-Publication Data record for this book is available from the British Library

ISBN 978-0-86037-627-9

Printed in Turkey by IMAK

ZAK and His Little LIES

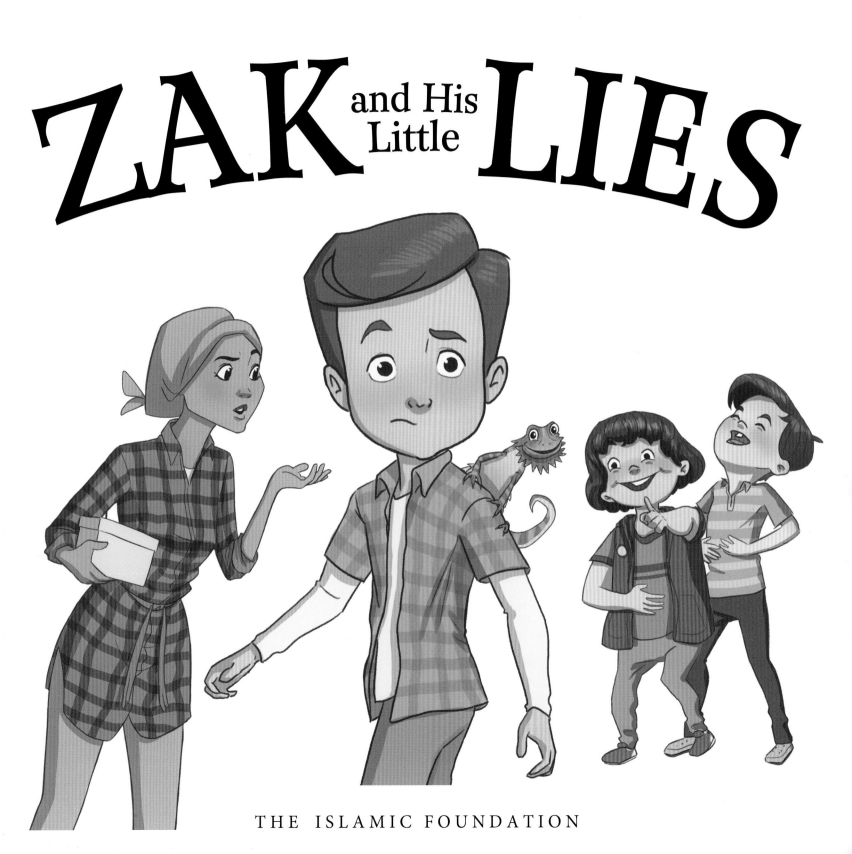

THE ISLAMIC FOUNDATION

Zak was having a great day. He only had one more chore to do—delivering baklava to some neighbours. After that, Baba had promised to take him and Hana to the new skateboard park.

"Zak!" his mother called from downstairs. "Make sure that the lid to Dwayne's terrarium is on tightly before leaving."

Zak looked at the terrarium. The lid was off, and Dwayne, his pet bearded dragon, was nowhere to be seen. "Dwayne," Zak whispered. "Wherever you are, stay here and be good."

"Zak, is Dwayne in his terrarium?" Mama asked as he was walking down the stairs.

Zak hesitated. He didn't want to tell his mama that Dwayne had escaped again. But he didn't want to lie either.

Zak thought about telling the truth...

...but instead he said, "Safe and sound."
Hana started to giggle.
"What's so funny?" Zak asked angrily.
Hana pointed to his shoulder. Dwayne was sitting there comfortably with a big grin on his face.

"What did Baba and I tell you about lying?" Mama asked. "If you lie one more time today, there will be no skateboard park later. Do you understand?"
Zak nodded. He knew his mama was right.
"Good," she said. "Please put Dwayne back. Then you and Hana can deliver these two boxes of baklava to the neighbours."

Zak ran to his room and quickly put Dwayne
back. He then hurried back downstairs,
excited to finish his last chore.
At the front door he grabbed a box of pastries
from his mama and jumped on his skateboard.

"Whatever you do kids, do not even go near Miss Martha's flowerbed," Mama said
as they were leaving. "She still hasn't forgotten when Dwayne ate her geraniums."

Their first stop was Mrs Clark's house.

Mrs Clark opened her door and Zak handed her a box of baklava.
"Mmm, these smell great." Mrs Clark said. "I'm sure you will raise a lot of money for your masjid with these. Hana, come with me and I'll give you the money. Zak, the boys are in the kitchen. I'm sure they'd love to see you."

Zak wasn't so sure he wanted to see them. Mrs Clark's sons were a few years older than Zak and they teased him a lot in school.

"Little Zakky!" one of the boys said when Zak walked into the kitchen. "I dare you to try one of my mum's famous jalapeño fireballs." He picked up a plate full of food and thrust it under Zak's nose.

Zak had never heard of a jalapeño fireball before, but it sounded hot and spicy. And he didn't like hot and spicy things at all. If he told the truth, the older boys would tease him. But he didn't want to lie because he really wanted to go to the new skateboard park.

Zak thought about telling the truth…

...but instead he said,
"I love fireballs!"
and grabbed the biggest jalapeño on
the plate, plopping it into his mouth.

As soon as he bit into it, he knew that he had made a BIG mistake.
He started to sweat. His eyes teared. His cheeks tingled. His tongue burned.
It felt like a volcano was erupting in his mouth.

"Ahhh," Zak screamed. The fireball was too hot to swallow so he ran outside to spit it out. He could hear the brothers laughing behind him.

Zak waited for Hana outside. He was embarrassed and upset. And it still felt like he was breathing fire. *Lying isn't good,* he thought.

"What's wrong with you? C'mon let's go!" Hana said when she saw him. She wanted to drop off the last box of baklava as quickly as possible to get to the new skateboard park. She was excited as well.

Zak jumped on his skateboard and followed Hana, who was almost running now.

Zak caught up with Hana at Miss Pat's letterbox. Suddenly they heard loud barking coming from her house. Zak froze.

"You're not still scared of dogs, are you?" Hana asked, a little surprised.

Zak had been terrified of dogs ever since a GIANT dog knocked him over when he was younger. If he told the truth, Hana would know that he was still afraid. But he didn't want to lie either because he really wanted to go to the new skateboard park.

Zak thought about telling the truth...

…but instead he said, "Not scared at all!"

Zak grabbed the pastry box from Hana, and headed for Miss Pat's front door without her. When he knocked on the door, the dog barked even louder.

"Back, Moose, back," Miss Pat yelled from inside.

As soon as Miss Pat opened the door, the dog BURST OUT.

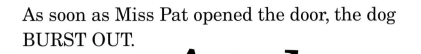

Zak dropped the pastry box and dashed straight for the slide at the side of the house. When he was safely at the top, he looked down to see the ferocious dog that was chasing him.

"Now, now, Moose. You shouldn't be scaring people," Miss Pat said as she picked up her little pooch and patted his head gently. "Here, honey. You don't want to leave without this." Miss Pat handed Zak some money and walked back inside.

"Not scared at all!" Hana said, as she approached Zak laughing.

Zak said nothing and slid down the slide. *Lying isn't good*, he thought as he walked to get his skateboard at the letterbox.

"I'll tell you what," Hana said. "I won't tell Mama that you lied about being scared of the little dog if you race me home."

Zak did not like to race Hana. She always won. But maybe he had a chance this time. He had his skateboard and she would be on foot. "I guess so," he said.

"Ready, Set, Go!" Hana said,

sprinting off down the pavement before
Zak had picked up his skateboard.

"That's not fair!" Zak yelled.
"I wasn't even ready!"

Zak jumped on his skateboard and chased after Hana. She was still in the lead when they were about a block away from home. But first they had to pass Miss Martha's flowerbed.

"You'd better slow down at the corner," Zak yelled to Hana.
"Remember what Mama said."

"Don't worry about me," Hana shouted back. "Watch this!"

Hana did a Grand Jete leap over Miss Martha's flowerbed like a prima ballerina. At precisely that moment, Miss Martha looked out her window to admire her flowers. Instead, she saw Hana soaring over her precious flowerbed! She did not wait to see where Hana landed. She ran to get her phone to call Hana's mother.

Zak, who was catching up, saw Hana land safely. She had not touched a single petal, but she was slowing down. He was sure that he could still beat her.

Suddenly, Dwayne seemed to appear out of nowhere, right in front of him.

"Watch out!" Zak screamed.

Zak swerved just in time, saving Dwayne. But he rolled straight through the middle of Miss Martha's beautiful flowers, leaving a very unfortunate path.

"Miss Martha just called me very upset," Mama said as soon as Zak walked in the door.

Uh oh, Zak thought. *I'm in trouble now.*

"She saw Hana leaping over her flowerbed and now her flowers are trampled. Hana said that she didn't touch them. Do you know what happened?"

Zak knew exactly what had happened. If he told the truth, he would get in BIG trouble. But he didn't want to lie either because he really wanted to go to the new skateboard park.

Zak thought about telling the truth…

...but instead he said, "Nope. I have no idea."

Zak walked up the stairs to his room. He heard Baba talking to Hana and Hana crying as he passed by her room. He felt terrible. *Lying isn't good,* he thought.

"I'm ready!" Baba burst into Zak's room. He was all decked out in skateboard gear, looking rather silly for a baba.

"Me too," Zak said glumly. Zak felt badly because of all the lies he had told that day, especially about Hana and the flowers.

"Why the sad face?" Baba asked.

Zak didn't want to tell his baba why he was so sad.

Zak thought about telling the truth…

…and he did!

He saw his Qur'an on his bookshelf and remembered the ayah, "Nothing in the earth and in the heavens is hidden from Allah." And Zak realized that even if his parents didn't know about all of his lies, Allah knew.

He also remembered what the Prophet Muhammad * had said about being truthful, especially that truthfulness leads to good deeds and good deeds lead to Jannah. Suddenly, going to the new skateboard park didn't seem that important anymore.

Zak told his baba everything that had happened that day, including all of his lies. When Zak was done, Baba said, "The truthful men and the truthful women, for them Allah has prepared forgiveness and a great reward."

Tears filled Zak's eyes. "I'm not one of the truthful," he said.

"Don't be sad," Baba said. "This ayah is about you. You told the truth about your lies. Allah is the Most Forgiving, Most Merciful. We should never lose hope in Allah's Mercy. Zak, how do you think you can make this right?"

Zak thought for a moment. "I can start by telling Mama and Hana the truth about the flowers, and then I have some neighbours to visit and a flowerbed to fix."

Zak smiled to himself. *Telling the truth feels great,* he thought as he led the way to Miss Martha's house.

Discussion Questions

What do you think Zak thought was more important than going to the new skateboard park at the end of the story?

What do you think Zak and his family are doing with all the gardening tools on the last page?

What do you think Zak is going to say when he visits Mrs Clark and her sons?

Did you ever feel like lying to belong? Not to be teased? To get out of trouble?

Sometimes lying might feel like the right thing to do at the time, but it isn't. If you are about to lie, what can you do to stop yourself?

Hana said that she wouldn't tell their parents that Zak had lied if he raced her home? That's not lying but was that good to do? Should she have told their parents that Zak had lied?

Do you know what the word taubah or "repent" means? If you do something wrong in Islam, Allah tells us to make taubah. How do you make taubah to Allah?

Why is it important to take care of your pet? Pets aren't toys; what does that mean? If someone is mistreating an animal, what would you do?